# Aladdin and the Lamp

Hilary Robinson and Andy Catling

W

# Chapter 1:
# Lazy Aladdin

There once lived a poor, lazy boy.
He spent the long, hot days playing in the
streets outside his house and sitting around
flicking stones into a pot.
His name was Aladdin.

One day, as Aladdin was playing in the yard, a stranger appeared. At first Aladdin was scared.

"Do not be scared of me," said the stranger. "I am your long-lost uncle and I am also a magician. Go now and tell your mother that I am here!"

Aladdin's mother had never heard of this
uncle, but she invited him to supper. He
seemed so kind that Aladdin's mother cried.
"Aladdin is such a lazy boy," she said.
"He will not work and he will not help me.
We have had no money since his father
died. We have very
little food to eat and
life is very hard."

The magician seemed to take pity on
Aladdin's mother and said to her, "Worry
not, for I have a plan and I may be able to
help you."

# Chapter 2:
# A Secret Cave

The next day, the magician led Aladdin up winding, dusty paths high into the mountains. As night drew in and the air became cold, they stopped to light a fire.

Aladdin watched as the magician threw some powder on to the glowing fire and chanted strange, magical words. Then, suddenly, the earth began to rumble and shake beneath their feet.

As if by magic, a heavy stone appeared out of the earth with a brass ring on top of it. "See this stone," said the magician. Aladdin nodded. "Well under this stone lies treasure, and that treasure will help to change both our lives. But I need your help.

"To lift this stone you must kneel before it and chant the names of your father and your grandfather. Only through those names and your voice do we have the power to enter the cave below."
Aladdin did as he was told.

The stone rolled away and opened up to
reveal a huge, dark hole in the ground.
The magician turned to Aladdin. "Now you
must go down those long, winding steps at
the end of which you will see a huge cave.
I need you to bring back to me the lamp
that is in the fruit garden. But you must
wear this ring at all times," he warned.

# Chapter 3:
# Finding Treasure

Aladdin walked through three great halls. They were filled with golden treasure, jewellery and sparkling stones. Never in his life had Aladdin seen such riches.

Then, he walked into bright sunshine as he arrived in a garden of trees heavily laden with ripe fruits. At the end of the garden was the lamp that the magician had told him about.

At once Aladdin grabbed it and ran back through the garden, through the caves and up the long, winding steps.

13

At the top of the steps the magician shouted at him. "Give me the lamp, boy! Give it to me now!"

"No I won't," shouted Aladdin. "I will only give it back to you when you get me out of here."

The magician was furious. He stamped on the ground. "You will suffer for this," he shouted and he threw more powder onto the fire. Then the stone rolled back, trapping Aladdin beneath it.

# Chapter 4:
# The Magic Ring

Alone in the cave, Aladdin was cold and scared. He realised that the man was not his uncle at all. The man was just a cunning magician who had lied to him and his mother, then used Aladdin to get hold of the lamp. "I wonder why he wants this old lamp?" thought Aladdin. "It doesn't look very precious!"

Aladdin twisted the ring on his finger as he thought. Then he jumped back in surprise as a genie rose up from out of the ring!

"Worry not!" said the genie. "I am the Genie of the Ring and I will obey you in all things," he said.

Aladdin was so shocked, he could barely
speak. "Please can you get me out of here?"
he begged. "It is dark and cold and
I have been trapped here by
a man who tricked me."

Suddenly, the earth opened up and the genie disappeared. Aladdin took his chance and escaped.

# Chapter 5:
# The Old Lamp

Back at home, Aladdin told his mother what
had happened and she hugged him tight.
"I am going to sell some cotton,"
she said, "for we have no
food left to eat.
With the
money, I will
be able to
buy us some
bread and we
can celebrate
your escape."

"No, there is no need," said Aladdin. "Keep your precious cotton for you will get more money if you sell this old lamp that I found. But it will need to be polished first."

As Aladdin's mother cleaned the lamp, she fell back in amazement. Another genie had appeared.

"Your wish is my command, master," said the genie to Aladdin. Now, Aladdin was getting used to making wishes!

"My wish," said Aladdin, "is for us to have some food. Please can you help my mother, for our cupboards are empty and we have no money for food."

The genie flew away and then returned
with four silver plates all heavily laden
with delicious food.

From that day on, all of Aladdin's wishes were
granted, and Aladdin made a lot of wishes!

Aladdin and his mother were able to live
in comfort, and Aladdin could be as lazy
as he pleased!

# About the story

*Aladdin* is a folk tale from the Middle East. Many people think that it was originally in the collection of stories called *One Thousand and One Nights* (often called *The Arabian Nights*) but it was only added to this collection in the 18th century CE by a French translator called Antoine Galland. Although the tale is Middle Eastern, the story seems to be set in China with mostly Muslim characters. Nowadays, the story has been made into films and is often performed as a pantomime with Aladdin's mother becoming the funny Widow Twanky. In the rest of this tale, Aladdin marries a princess and has many more adventures with the genies!

# Be in the story!

Imagine you are the magician. You have come back to Aladdin's town and found out he is now rich! What might you be thinking?

Now imagine you are Aladdin's mother. What do you want to say to the magician when he returns? And what do you want to say to your son, Aladdin?

First published in 2014 by
Franklin Watts
338 Euston Road
London
NW1 3BH

Franklin Watts Australia
Level 17/207 Kent Street
Sydney
NSW 2000

A CIP catalogue record for this book is available
from the British Library.

The artwork for this story first appeared in
Hopscotch Adventures: Aladdin and the Lamp

ISBN 978 1 4451 3377 5 (hbk)
ISBN 978 1 4451 3378 2 (pbk)
ISBN 978 1 4451 3380 5 (library ebook)
ISBN 978 1 4451 3379 9 (ebook)

Series Editor: Jackie Hamley
Series Advisor: Catherine Glavina
Series Designer: Cathryn Gilbert

Printed in China

Franklin Watts is a divison of
Hachette Children's Books,
an Hachette UK company.
www.hachette.co.uk